MW00906139

CONTENTS

WAITING

PREDICT

What do you think this story will be about? What helped you form your opinion?

Penn stood outside the command centre doors, shifting nervously from one foot to the other. She straightened her blue tunic then ran her hands over her shaven head. She hated waiting. Waiting was such a waste of time.

Behind the doors, the Earth Defence Committee was meeting to decide who would be the commander of the new Moon Security outpost.

But what was taking them so long? Surely it was an easy decision. The simulators held the records for every captain's training battles. The win-loss totals were available to everyone. Penn's totals were the best, so the decision was simple. Clearly she would make the best commander – or so she thought.

EARTH DE

CLEARLY
E WOULD
AKE THE BES
OMMANDER...

intern file 002–11.6.008'74c

What inferences can you make about Penn from the visual images and text relating to her character?

VISUAL FEATURES

...E CENTRE

...ai was **good,** too.

He must be her closest rival. There was no doubt he'd make an excellent commander. His battle plans were thorough, logical and sometimes adventurous, but... his damaged and lost ship numbers were high – too high. That had to count against him.

CLARIFY

outpost
simulators
logical

She **let** out a **sigh.**

She just wished the committee would hurry up and decide.

3

BEYOND
THE TEXT

Does the fictional scenario developed by the author have any parallels with current efforts to protect the world's resources? Why/why not?

Landing Bay 3 cam 6

4

Determined Security Contingency 90.97% - Oper
Evaluation response ID# - OS 726-690-A3D5

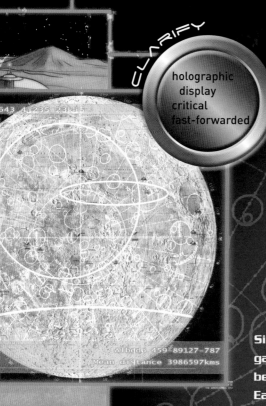

CLARIFY

holographic
display
critical
fast-forwarded

Penn wandered over to a screen on the far wall and stared at the holographic display of the new Moon outpost.

Even though she had looked at it many times before, there was always something different to see. On the screen, the four domed buildings rotated and opened up. Cameras zoomed in and out, showing the living quarters, workshops, food gardens, docking stations and the operations centre, with flashing satellite images of the Moon and Earth. The outpost had been finished three years ahead of schedule.

Since the starway through the Milky Way galaxy had opened up, Earth's security had become critical. Minerals taken from the Earth's core were key ingredients in morphlo – the fuel that had given humans star travel. The morphlo minerals weren't renewable, so all reserves had to be protected.

Satellite and probe sensors had recorded alien vessels sailing close to the solar system's protected space. No doubt some of them had scanned the planets. It was only a matter of time before there was contact. But would the contact be friendly or hostile? No one knew. So the building of the new Moon defence outpost was fast-forwarded.

Penn sighed again and cracked her knuckles.

Suddenly, the light tubes on the wall above her flashed green and the doors slicked open.
Penn took a deep breath, straightened her tunic again and stepped forward. This was it.

Why do you think the author introduced the security issues facing Earth early in the story?

AUTHOR
PURPOSE

The command centre was dark, except for a single light shining on a simulator chair in the middle of the room. "Take the chair, Captain."

Penn recognised Chairman Hind's deep voice. She sat down and the chair's soft synthetic seemed to swallow her. Her hands and fingers moved easily over the familiar sensor pads set into the armrests. The large simulator screen in front of her was blank. Behind her, in the darkness, she felt eyes watching her.

"Captain," said Chairman Hind, "we have reviewed your records, training schedules and battle simulations.

Your results are outstanding, but the Moon outpost commander's position cannot be decided on a battle win-loss record alone. The Moon outpost will be Earth's first line of defence. The new commander must be logical, intuitive, experienced and imaginative. You fit those criteria, but so does another captain. Therefore, the Defence Committee has agreed that the new commander's position will be decided by one last battle simulation – a battle that will test all your skills and abilities.

Captain, you know the procedure. You may begin."

CLARIFY

synthetic
intuitive
criteria
strategies

Penn felt her breathing quicken. That's not fair, she thought. She was the best captain. She deserved the promotion. She clenched her teeth. She wanted to shout at the committee, to tell them that they were wrong, but she knew any show of anger or frustration would count against her. Anyway, the delay could be deliberate – just part of the whole process.

Simile/Metaphor/Personification/Alliteration
What literary devices has the author used?
What was his purpose for using these
devices? How did it help your understanding
of the atmosphere created by the committee?

LANGUAGE
FEATURES

She breathed easier. Okay, she thought.
No decision for the new commander has
been made. And the other captain being
considered has to be Lai.

Am I going first? Does the best go
first? Am I setting the standard
for Lai? She shook her head,
blocking the wasteful thoughts,
and concentrated on the necessary
preparations.

She thought back over her recent battles. In her mind, she saw hundreds of
battleship formations spread across space. She'd never lost a battle. She had
always won because the other captains didn't shift from the
strategies of the instruction models built into the simulators. Their
moves were predictable and easily blocked, but hers were always
inventive and totally unexpected.

Every enemy had weaknesses. Her goal in each
battle was to find a weakness and attack it
before the same was done to her. It was a
simple strategy, but it worked. And in the
final battle, she would use it again to prove
once and for all that she was the best.

"Captain," said the chairman,
"the committee is waiting."

ANALYSE

What inferences can you make
about the way the command
centre was set up for the battle
simulation? What effect could this
have on the contestants for the
command post?

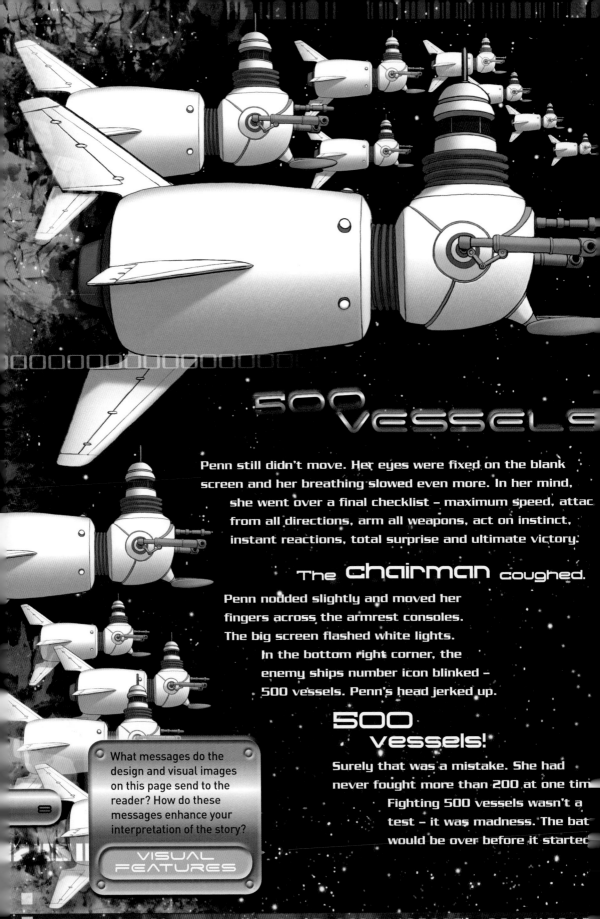

500 VESSELS

Penn still didn't move. Her eyes were fixed on the blank screen and her breathing slowed even more. In her mind, she went over a final checklist – maximum speed, attac from all directions, arm all weapons, act on instinct, instant reactions, total surprise and ultimate victory.

The **Chairman** coughed.

Penn nodded slightly and moved her fingers across the armrest consoles. The big screen flashed white lights. In the bottom right corner, the enemy ships number icon blinked – 500 vessels. Penn's head jerked up.

500 vessels!

Surely that was a mistake. She had never fought more than 200 at one tim Fighting 500 vessels wasn't a test – it was madness. The bat would be over before it startec

What messages do the design and visual images on this page send to the reader? How do these messages enhance your interpretation of the story?

VISUAL FEATURES

9045 095691kt 6o35 ; 34j5 0824 495805ww234545345

CLARIFY

ultimate

"The **enemy** has **500 vessels?**" **she said** out loud.

But there was no response from the committee. Penn shrugged and almost grinned. They were playing her at her own game. They had done the unexpected – caught her by surprise. But she wouldn't be caught off guard again.

Onscreen, the enemy fleet was stationary. Nothing would move until she activated her ships – just four flights of thirty cruisers. Penn knew she didn't have a choice. If she wanted the commander's job, she had to fight, even though everything was unequal. She rolled her shoulders back and forth to relax them, took a deep breath, then tapped and slid her fingers over the consoles. The big screen turned green then black and her cruisers entered the battle space from the four corners.

FIGHTING 500 VESSELS WASN'T A TEST – IT WAS MADNESS!

OPINION

Do you think the battle simulation Penn is facing is fair? Why/why not? What would you do in the same circumstances?

CHARACTER ANALYSIS

What inferences can you make about Penn from her decision to fight on despite the odds?

Penn noticed that one enemy ship was larger than all the others and that the many smaller ships seemed to form a loose, random barrier around it. The larger ship glowed a bit brighter and moved in a regular pattern that suggested it was the fleet controller. Penn decided it had to be the mother ship. It would be her target. With luck, once it was destroyed, the enemy's battle plan would fall apart.

Penn kept her cruisers in simulator formation – a tight V-shape – and moved them slowly towards the large ship. As the cruisers edged closer, she changed one flight into a more streamlined bullet-shaped formation then suddenly slapped two panels on the consoles.

The cruisers thrust forwards, directly towards the mother ship, then retreated just as quickly. Penn knew that sudden, random movements and changes in formation confused computer simulations. One by one, she brought in the other flights of cruisers until there were four bullet-shaped formations rushing towards the mother ship, then retreating. Confused, the enemy fighters withdrew, forming a tighter and tighter shield around their command vessel.

Has the author effectively described the battle simulation and the mood and atmosphere surrounding it? Why/why not?

SETTING

ATTACK!

When the cruisers had moved within firing range, Penn halted the formations and held them in a stationary position for a moment. Then she suddenly separated all the cruisers and sent them rushing among the enemy. She worked the panels, dials and pads fast, manoeuvring the ships left, right, up and down.

They **dodged**, dipped, swerved, rolled, **looped**, **Flipped** and stalled.

Penn didn't activate any weapons. She worked hard to create a jumbled mess of whizzing, darting ships that cleverly worked their way beyond the enemy defence lines. Confused and disorganised, the fighters had to turn inwards to chase the cruisers.

They were smaller, faster and more nimble than Penn's bigger ships, but their weapons were useless. If they fired on the cruisers, they risked hitting the mother ship, too.

Penn knew the advantage wouldn't last long. With their superior speed, the fighters were gaining fast and were almost back in clear space between the cruisers and the mother ship.

BEYOND THE TEXT

Can you relate to how Penn is feeling as she "plays the game"? What connections can you make?

13

Penn flicked her fingers across a set of lighted panels. The cruisers regrouped into four flights then streaked towards the mother ship.

The fighters drew level before slowly going one ship length ahead of the cruisers. Then two ship lengths. Then three. With their red tracking beam lights burning brightly, the fighters turned back towards the cruisers.

Then, just before they straightened into a head-on flight path, Penn hit the all-fire pads on the consoles.

She hit them hard, again and again.

Nothing happened for a moment. Then, slowly, almost sluggishly, five continuous bolts of light shot away from the cruisers, flashed across space and thumped into the mother ship. The huge vessel reared up, shuddered, trembled, then stabilised and began to swell and bubble.

Its outer layer blistered and bulged, then separated and peeled away. Suddenly, the simulator screen exploded in bright, pulsing light, blinding Penn.

She shut her eyes and turned away.

When she looked back, the mother ship had burst apart, vanishing inside great plumes of smoke, gas, flying debris and dazzling brightness. She watched the eruption grow outwards.

No fighter or cruiser seemed able to escape the white-hot blossoming clouds. The raging fireballs engulfed fleet after fleet of ships.

SYMBOLISM

Why has the author introduced the disintegration of the enemy here? Do you think there is also a symbolic meaning contained in this reference? Why/why not?

ITS OUTER
LAYER BLISTERED
AND BULGED
THEN SEPARATED
AND PEELED
AWAY

Penn watched until the mighty blast
faded to smaller, separate, glowing lumps
of red, yellow and orange gases.

Then she sat back in the chair
and smiled to herself. What
had seemed an impossible
task had been rather simple.
She waited for the
overhead lights to come
on, but the room stayed
dark and no one from
the committee spoke.
Then the ship number
icon flashed across the
screen. Enemy ships – 1.
Home ships – 1.

Penn **stared**
at the words.
The battle **was** over...
surely?

What do you think
will happen now in
the storyline?

PLOT

CLARIFY

stabilised

15

ONE ON ONE

A lone enemy fighter hovered in the top right corner, but there was no cruiser icon. Frowning, Penn touched the console. MANUAL CONTROL ONLY blinked across the screen.

"What..." Penn looked around, but the **room** was still **dark.**

CLARIFY

drawn-out

"I won," she said. "You put me up against a ridiculous number of enemy ships and I beat them. I passed your test. I proved once and for all that I am the Defence Force's best captain."

She turned and peered into the darkness. "One ship is left. Big deal. What is one ship compared to 500?"

Still the committee didn't speak. Had they even heard her? Why were they making her duel with the last fighter? What was the point?

She touched the console again. MANUAL CONTROL ONLY – ACTIVATE COLUMN scrolled across the screen.

Why do you think the committee fails to respond to Penn's questions?

QUESTION

Penn shook her head. She couldn't hide her frustration any longer but she was beyond caring.

"I just destroyed 499 invading vessels," she muttered, "and they want me to fight one more. **Ridiculous! Petty! Unreasonable!"**

She hit the console pad again. A control column rose out of the floor in front of her. She grabbed it roughly and her cruiser appeared onscreen. She hit the console harder this time and the big screen became the cruiser's cockpit, complete with dials, pads, buttons, levers and screens. Penn was the pilot.

A small screen directly in front of her buzzed and the enemy fighter came into view behind her. Penn eased her grip on the control column, moved it backwards and felt the cruiser pick up speed.

Simile/Metaphor/Personification/Alliteration
What literary devices has the author used?
How did it help your understanding?

LANGUAGE FEATURES

"I JUST DESTROYED 499 INVADING VESSELS"

Alien Vessel ID
Q5632 37989134:
Class=Fighter
Attack Status
Vital I
0#873 Kholjsf/
2q983764521342

ANALYSE

"I just destroyed 499 invading vessels and they want me to fight one more."

What inferences can you make from this statement about Penn's ability to divorce her real world from the cyber world? What serious consequences could result from an inability to relate to reality?

Although one part of her was annoyed at having to fight on, another part didn't mind. A big battle like the one she had just won was like a giant jigsaw. No battle or puzzle can be completed without patience, concentration and an ability to see where each ship or piece fits into the big picture. A big battle is intense, drawn-out and complex, whereas a one-on-one duel is usually exciting, fast, uncomplicated and fun.

Penn touched the booster pad and whispered,

"Game on."

The cruiser climbed. Up. Up. Up. The fighter followed. Penn rammed the column forward. The cruiser dived. She tapped in the speed injectors. Warp one... faster. Warp two... faster. Warp three... still faster. The fighter followed, just out of firing range. Penn frowned and licked her lips.

"I have to **shake** it off," she breathed.

Debris from the mother ship explosion appeared on her port side. She swung the cruiser high and wide, eased the column back, then wove among the bits of broken ships. A few pieces bounced off her deflector shields into the path of the fighter, forcing it to change course. Penn immediately shoved the column forward and hauled the cruiser to the left in a short, tight loop.

Now she was behind the fighter. But not for long. The fighter was faster and more nimble. It spurted forward and turned in a tight arc. Penn tried to follow, but her bigger ship shuddered and shook. The turn was too tight. She couldn't control it.

Penn eased off the injectors and took the cruiser into a steep climb. The cockpit screen squealed. The fighter was back on her tail and in firing range. Penn grunted. Whoever had programmed the fighter was good. Very good.

She pulled the cruiser to the left, threw it back to the right, then rolled it over. Swerve. Roll. Swerve. Roll. And the fighter followed.

Penn felt sweat trickle down her back. She shifted in her chair. "I've got to get away... somehow," she muttered. "Shake it off! Think! Do the inventive... the unexpected!"

CLARIFY

deflector shields

SWERVE.
ROLL

SWERVE
ROLL

How does the author's use of language change as the tension builds in the final one-on-one fight?

LANGUAGE
FEATURE

ESCAPE

Then she smiled. She remembered an escape trick she'd used against a faster ship another time. If it worked again, it would be once only. But, with luck, once would be enough.

Penn eased the column back, slowing the cruiser and bringing the fighter even closer. She saw its tracking beams' bright red lights before she heard them flashing and flickering around her. She had just seconds before she was fired upon. "A little closer," she whispered, as the fighter's sharp, blackened nose filled her cockpit screen.

"Just a **fraction more**... now!"

How has the author stereotyped Penn? Has this influenced your perception of Penn? Why/why not?

STEREOTYPE

Penn hauled the control column back. The cruiser jolted to a stop and hovered. There was nowhere for the fighter to go except up. It skimmed overhead, its underbelly just missing the cruiser. Flicking and weaving and wobbling, it tried to slow down while Penn thrust the column forward again and tapped in the speed injectors.

CHARACTER ANALYSIS

Summarise what you know about Penn, using evidence from the text and the inferences you have made.

Evidence from Text	Inferential Information

Within seconds, the cruiser was back up to warp three. The slowing fighter was dead ahead and in firing range. Penn stabbed the glowing fire pad on the column with both her thumbs and the cruiser's tracking beams criss-crossed the small gap. One locked on to the fighter. The fire pad glowed again and Penn hit it hard. A bright, white light bolt thumped into the fighter and it jerked and wobbled, then dipped, spun and spiralled downwards.

Down. Down. Down.
And Penn followed.

Another tracking beam locked on to the fighter. Penn hit the fire pad again. More light bolts hit the fighter. This time it reared up and began to swell and bubble. Its outer layer blistered and bulged, then separated and peeled away, as it had on the mother ship.

Suddenly, the cockpit screen exploded in bright, pulsing light, but Penn had already turned away. When she looked back, the fighter was glowing silvery-white. Then it rolled over and burst into flames and smoke and dazzling brightness.

Penn watched until the blast faded to a tiny shining cloud, then she eased the control column back and brought the cruiser to a stop.

The cockpit screen went blank for a moment, then large red letters scrolled across the screen –

Game Over!

Jargon – words and phrases used by a particular group or culture that are often not understood by other people. Can you find any examples?

LANGUAGE FEATURES

BURST INTO FLAMES AND SMOKE AND DAZZLING BRIGHTNESS

Why do you think science-fiction authors sometimes use jargon as a tool?

QUESTION

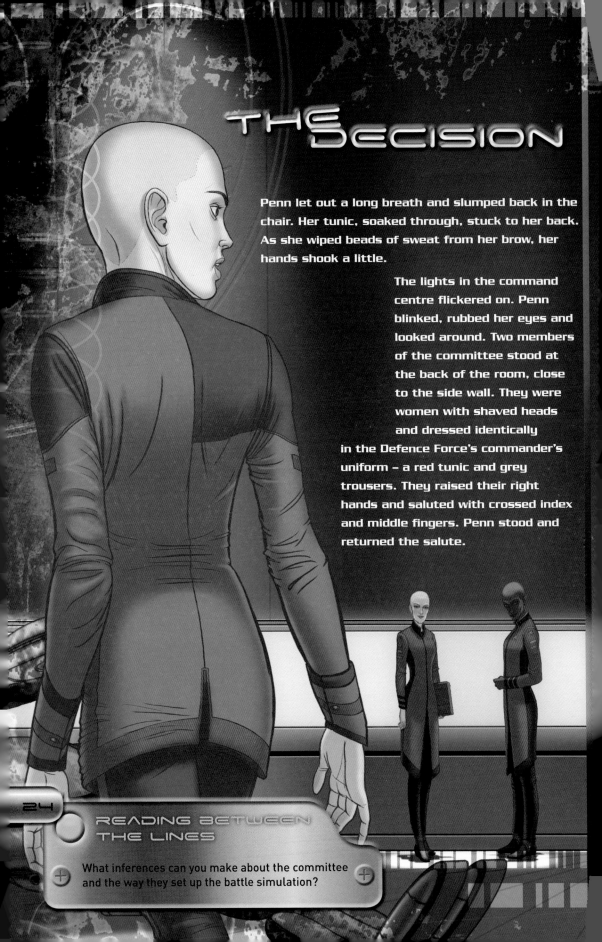

THE DECISION

Penn let out a long breath and slumped back in the chair. Her tunic, soaked through, stuck to her back. As she wiped beads of sweat from her brow, her hands shook a little.

The lights in the command centre flickered on. Penn blinked, rubbed her eyes and looked around. Two members of the committee stood at the back of the room, close to the side wall. They were women with shaved heads and dressed identically in the Defence Force's commander's uniform – a red tunic and grey trousers. They raised their right hands and saluted with crossed index and middle fingers. Penn stood and returned the salute.

READING BETWEEN THE LINES

What inferences can you make about the committee and the way they set up the battle simulation?

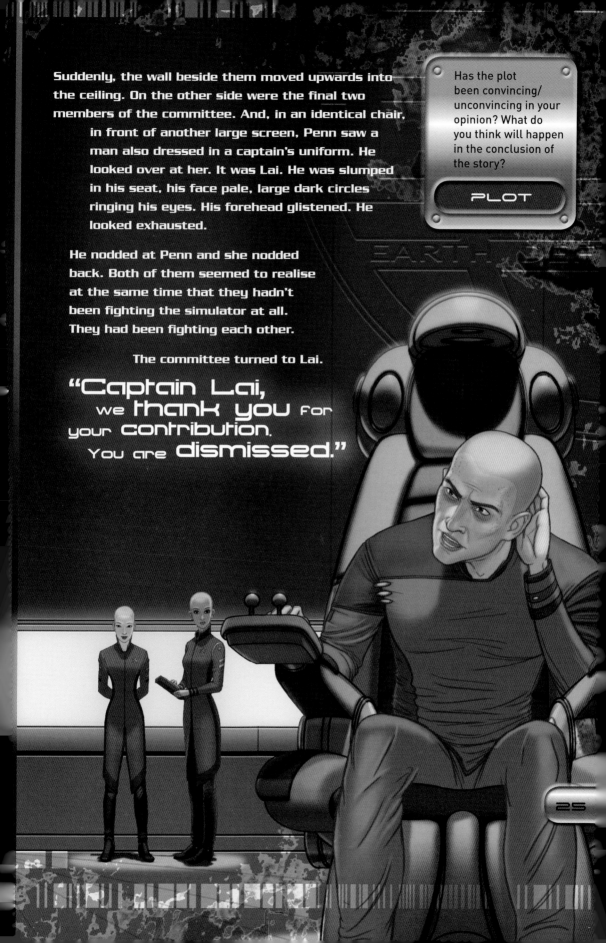

Suddenly, the wall beside them moved upwards into the ceiling. On the other side were the final two members of the committee. And, in an identical chair, in front of another large screen, Penn saw a man also dressed in a captain's uniform. He looked over at her. It was Lai. He was slumped in his seat, his face pale, large dark circles ringing his eyes. His forehead glistened. He looked exhausted.

He nodded at Penn and she nodded back. Both of them seemed to realise at the same time that they hadn't been fighting the simulator at all. They had been fighting each other.

The committee turned to Lai.

"Captain Lai, we thank you for your contribution. You are dismissed."

Has the plot been convincing/unconvincing in your opinion? What do you think will happen in the conclusion of the story?

PLOT

How credible was the futuristic setting for this story? In your opinion, what details made the setting believable/ unbelievable?

SETTING

Penn watched Lai leave his chair slowly and shuffle out through the doors. Thoughts raced through her mind. Why had the committee made her and Lai fight? Why was the fight so unequal? And what would have happened had she lost? Was a rematch planned with the odds stacked in her favour? She wanted answers but, before she could speak, the committee walked around to the front of her screen.

PERSONAL RESPONCE

What helped you relate to the events in this story?

"What you have just experienced was unfair, one-sided and perhaps even cruel," said Chairman Hind. "But, at any time, a commander of the Moon outpost may also be massively outnumbered by invading aliens. The committee had to be sure that you would be successful against overwhelming odds. We also had to be sure that you were capable of staging a large, victorious battle plan as well as manipulating an individual fighter ship. Your skills are impressive, Captain."

Chairman Hind glanced at the three other committee members. When they nodded, she smiled and said, "Congratulations. Please approach the committee to receive your commander's tunic."

Penn smiled, too. At last, she thought. At last!

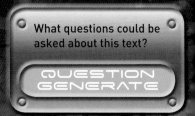

What questions could be asked about this text?

QUESTION GENERATE

THINK ABOUT THE TEXT

MAKING CONNECTIONS

What connections can you make to the characters, plot, setting and themes of GAME OVER?

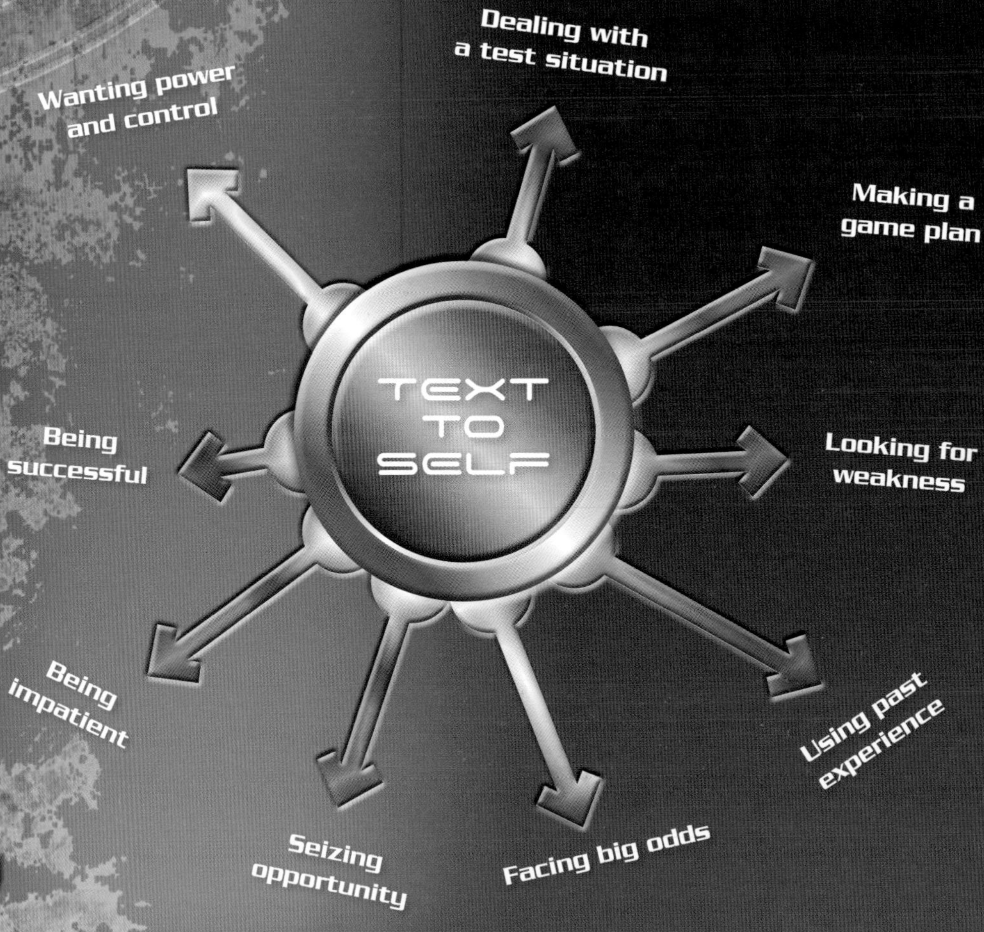

Dealing with a test situation

Wanting power and control

Making a game plan

Being successful

TEXT TO SELF

Looking for weakness

Being impatient

Seizing opportunity

Facing big odds

Using past experience

TEXT TO TEXT/MEDIA

Talk about texts/media you have read, listened to or seen that have similar themes and compare the treatment of theme and the differing author styles.

TEXT TO WORLD

Talk about situations in the world that might connect to elements in the story.

PLANNING A SCIENCE-FICTION STORY

Think about What Defines Science Fiction

Science fiction is set in an imaginary world of the future. The situations and events feature more or less feasible scientific advances that have created a different society or way of life.

1 Think about the Plot

Introduce an event in a futuristic world that presents a problem or conflict and bring in the characters that the event affects.

Decide on an event to draw the reader into your story. What will the main conflict/problem be?

Build your story to a turning point. This is the most exciting/suspenseful part of the story.

Climax

Conflict

Falling Action

Rising Action

Set the scene: who is the story about? When and where is it set?

Decide on a final event that will resolve the conflict/problem and bring your story to a close.

Introduction

Resolution

Explore:

- how characters from the
  futuristic time frame
  think, feel and act

- what might motivate their behaviour

- how their language incorporates "technological speak"

- the social structures (of family/
  communities) that typecast character
  status, appearance and behaviour.

3 Decide on the Setting

Atmosphere/mood   ⟶   location   ⟶   time

Use predictions of scientific advances and your imagination to make your setting feasible.

WRITING A SCIENCE-FICTION STORY

Have you . . .

- Exposed how technology affects the hopes and anxieties of characters in the futuristic world?

- Been true to the context of your time frame?

- Provided a window on the future?

- Explored values and beliefs of the time?

- Developed events that might be feasible?

- Used scientific "dressing" to clothe the fantasy content?

...don't forget to revisit your writing. Do you need to change, add or delete anything to improve your story?